The Secret of the Old Mill

written by Jill Atkins

Illustrated by Amy Lane

Chapter 1

Cassie ran ahead of Grandad and pushed open the library door.

The Secret of the Old Mill

'The Secret of the Old Mill'
An original concept by Jill Atkins
© Jill Atkins 2022

Illustrated by Amy Lane

Published by MAVERICK ARTS PUBLISHING LTD
Studio 11, City Business Centre, 6 Brighton Road,
Horsham, West Sussex, RH13 5BB
© Maverick Arts Publishing Limited August 2022
+44 (0)1403 256941

A CIP catalogue record for this book is available at the British Library.

ISBN 978-1-84886-911-0

www.maverickbooks.co.uk

This book is rated as: Lime Band (Guided Reading)

"I'll see you later," Grandad said as Cassie headed for the fiction shelves. "I want to find a book about photography."

Cassie smiled. Grandad was mad about photography.

It was a big library and there were rows and rows of books for her age group. She liked scary books best, especially ghost stories.

She walked slowly along the line of books. Suddenly, she stopped and stared as she read the spine of one of them. The author's name stood out as if it was lit up. It was *her* name: Cassandra Florakis! The book was called *The Secret of the Old Mill.*

She pulled it out and looked at the front cover. Her stomach clenched. The picture was of a girl who looked exactly like her! And in the background, there was an old mill like the one close to where she lived.

Quickly, Cassie sat down in the corner, opened the book and began to read.

Cassandra leapt up from her chair as she heard the knock on the door. She knew it would be Grandad. He always came round on Saturdays so they could go to the library.

Cassie gasped and read it again. That was just like her and her grandad!

Grandad came inside. "Are you ready?" he asked.

"Yes," said Cassandra, pulling on her jacket.

At that moment, her big brother, Hector, came downstairs two at a time. He was very tall and dark-haired, and towered over Cassandra and Grandad.

Cassie couldn't believe it. She had a big brother called Hector too. He was eighteen and could drive.

Cassandra and Grandad climbed into Grandad's car and set off.

After a few minutes, Grandad paused when they reached the old mill.

He stared at it. The sails were still. The mill had not been used to grind flour for many years. Then he drove to the library...

"Ready to go?" Grandad's voice snapped Cassie out of the story.

She looked up. He was holding a book called *Night Photography*.

She nodded, but couldn't speak. She was still in shock. It was uncanny! How could there possibly be a book that exactly mirrored everything about her?

Chapter 2

As soon as they were home, Cassie ran up to her room and opened the book. She quickly finished the chapter then, turning to the next page, she read on:

Cassandra loved her bedroom with its brightly painted walls, overflowing bookcase and high cabin bed with a desk underneath.

Cassie stopped reading and stared around her. It was exactly as described in the book! As she read on, she saw how much Cassandra's world matched hers: the street where she lived; the town; even the school. She laughed at the description of her teacher with his round face and glasses. She gasped when she saw the names of her two best friends: Monica and Serap!

"Cassie!" called her mum from downstairs. "Stop reading now and spend some time outside."

"In a minute," Cassie replied, but she couldn't leave the book. It was too fascinating!

Suddenly, there was a flash that almost blinded Cassandra. It was quickly followed by the crash of thunder. Rain began to cascade down like a waterfall.

Cassandra was worried. Hector had a football match this afternoon and Grandad was going out with his camera. She hoped they were sheltering from the storm.

Cassie was so deep in the story that she didn't notice the weather. But then she realised she could hardly see the words on the page. The sky outside had become very dark. She frowned. Like in the book, Hector had gone to play football and Grandad would be out taking photos.

At that moment, there was a flash and a loud rumble. Heavy rain began.

"This book is so amazing," Cassie said to herself. "How can it possibly be? It seems to be telling me what's going to happen!"

Chapter 3

When Hector came in later that afternoon, he was soaked. His dark hair was stuck to his head and he was very muddy.

"That was some storm," he said.

"I guessed it would come," said Cassie, looking up from her book.

"Really? How?" asked Hector with a frown.

Cassie held up the book.

"I read about it in here," she said.

"What do you mean?" he asked.

"It's weird. It's all about me... and you... and

Grandad..."

"That's silly," said Hector. "How can that be?"

"I'll show you," said Cassie.

She flicked the pages of the book and found the part about the storm. Hector peered at it. Then he laughed.

"So what?" he said. "Just because there was a storm in your book..."

"But I'd only just read this part when the storm started here," Cassie interrupted. "Anyway, I haven't told you the rest."

Hector shook his head.

"Not now," he said, heading for the door. "I'd better get cleaned up."

Cassie sighed. Hector wasn't interested. He had even laughed. He didn't believe what an amazing book this was.

At that moment, Grandad arrived. He was soaked too. Cassie ran to fetch him a towel.

"I've been out with my camera," Grandad said.

"I know," said Cassie.

"I was taking some brilliant pictures of birds...
but then the rain came. The lens got steamed up
so it was useless."

Cassie didn't tell Grandad about how
extraordinary her book was. She didn't want him
to laugh like Hector. Maybe she could share it
with Monica and Serap at school on Monday. She
hoped they would believe her.

Chapter 4

It rained all day on Sunday, but Cassie didn't mind. As long as she had finished her homework, Mum let her carry on with reading the story. She curled up in an armchair and read on.

It was Monday, and Cassandra rushed into the school playground and met up with Monica and Serap. The bell rang for lessons so they didn't have time to chat. They were halfway through the first lesson, when a piercing alarm sounded—the fire alarm. It made Cassandra jump.

"Right, everyone," called Mr Owens. "You know what to do. We've practised this. No talking. No running. Everyone out into the playground."

Cassandra hurried with the rest of her class and stood in the row with her friends. She stared at the school building. Was it on fire? She couldn't see any flames or even smell smoke.

After half an hour of waiting, the Head called everyone back inside.

"It was a very small fire," she said. "It's out now. Don't worry."

Cassandra felt relieved as she followed the rest of the class. It would have been a catastrophe if the school had burnt down!

Now Cassie *definitely* couldn't wait to tell her friends about the book!

★★★

On Monday morning, she rushed over to Monica and Serap, but the bell rang before she could say anything. As they reached the classroom, Cassie wondered if the fire alarm would go off today just like it had in the book.

In the middle of the lesson, the fire bell rang loudly. Her heart jolted.

"It's only a small fire," she said as they filed out. "We don't need to worry. They'll put it out straight away."

"How do you know that?" asked Serap.

"It's exactly like in a book I've been reading," answered Cassie.

"But that's only a story," said Monica.

"No talking in the line," called Mr Owens.

"I'll tell you at break," whispered Cassie.

After half an hour of waiting, the Head announced that the fire had been dealt with.

"It was only a small fire," she said. "But it's out now. Don't worry."

Monica and Serap stared at Cassie with open mouths.

"Told you so!" whispered Cassie.

At break, Cassie told them all about the book.

"Wow! That's amazing!" exclaimed Monica.

"Can I read it after you?" asked Serap.

Cassie smiled to herself. She knew her friends would believe her!

Chapter 5

After school, the first thing Cassie did was run up to her room. She opened the book at the next chapter.

Cassandra's grandad called in that evening.

"I'm going to the old mill," he announced. "I want to take some photos at sunset."

"I've heard the place is haunted," laughed Hector. "Mind you don't meet any ghosts."

Grandad grinned. "You never know," he said.

He drove out to the old mill and parked beside it. He took a few photos of the mill then opened the creaky, old door and went in. It was darker inside. He climbed a ladder to the upper floor. In front of him he saw cogs that turned when the wind blew the sails.

Suddenly, he heard a creaking sound.

He froze. Was that the ghost that people talked about? Were the sails turning?

Just then, a white shape drifted through the air in front of him. Lifting his camera quickly, he slipped and fell against the cogs.

His foot fell through a gap in the floorboards. He was trapped!

Cassie felt her body tighten with tension as she wondered what was going to happen next. She turned the page. Nothing! A blank page!

"Oh no!" she cried.

She hurriedly flicked through the rest of the book. All the pages were blank! She wouldn't be able to find out. What if the same thing was happening to *her* grandad?

She closed the book and ran downstairs.

"Hector," she cried. "I think Grandad is in trouble!"

"Why do you think that?"

"Well, in my book..." she said.

"Oh, not that again!" moaned Hector.

"But the Grandad in the book has fallen at the old mill..." she cried.

"It's just a coincidence..." he argued.

"No it isn't!"

"You expect me to believe all this rubbish?" asked Hector. "A book can't tell you what's going to happen."

Cassie put her hands on her hips.

"Well, I have evidence," she shouted. "I knew about the storm while you were out in it. And I knew that the fire alarm at school was going to go off, but it was only a small fire. And now, I've just read that Grandad is in trouble."

"Hmm," muttered Hector.

"And Grandad is interested in the old mill," said Cassie. "People say it's haunted. He's gone there to take photos. Please can we go and make sure he's alright?"

Hector sighed.

"Okay," he said. "Let's go."

Cassie fidgeted in her seat as Hector drove to the old mill.

"Look!" she shouted as they arrived. "There's his car."

But there was no sign of Grandad.

Chapter 6

Cassie stayed close to Hector as they began their search. She shuddered. The mill was really creepy and dark. She heard creaking and a moaning sound. Was that the ghost? Hector switched on his torch.

At that moment, a white shape drifted across in front of them.

Cassie screamed and gripped Hector's arm.

Then she heard another sound in the distance. It was a voice.

"Help!"

"It's Grandad!" she gasped.

"Quick! Let's find him."

Cassie noticed the ladder.

"Up there!" she said.

She climbed up first and Hector shone the torch so she could see ahead.

"Grandad!" she cried when she saw him.

"Thank goodness you came," he said. "I slipped. My leg is stuck."

Hector managed to free Grandad's leg. Luckily, it wasn't broken.

The white shape drifted across the room again.

Cassie opened her mouth to scream, but Grandad held up his hand.

"Don't scare it," he said. "Look, it's a barn owl. I knew it was here. I wanted to take photos of its nest. There are chicks."

"Chicks! So that's the secret of the old mill!" gasped Cassie. "I thought it was a ghost!"

"I suspected that at first," said Grandad. "Thanks for coming to rescue me. How did you know I was here?"

"It's all in that book I got out from the library," Cassie told him.

Hector grinned. "It's some weird book," he admitted.

"And I can't wait to finish it!" she said.

Cassie helped Grandad down the ladder then he hobbled to Hector's car. When they arrived home, Cassie looked closely at Grandad's ankle.

It was quite swollen so she fetched some ice from the freezer, placed it on his ankle and wrapped it in a towel. Then she ran up to her room. She hoped there would be more to read.

But the rest of the pages were still blank.

She frowned, disappointed. It was not going to tell her any more about the future. In the end, she decided to take it back to the library.

★★★

At school, she told her friends about Grandad's adventure and how the book had foretold it.

"Wow!" said Monica. "So what happened at the end of the book?"

"That was the strange part," said Cassie. "Nothing! The pages were blank so I took it back to the library."

"What a pity," said Monica.

"Oh, I would have liked to have seen it... Can we get it out again?" asked Serap. "I think it's really fascinating."

On Saturday, the three friends went to look for it together. They searched the shelves, but the book seemed to have vanished!

But all at once, Serap squealed.

"Look!" she said. "That's my name!"

Cassie leaned forward and read the spine of the book Serap was pointing at. It was *The Mystery of the Lake* by Serap Unel!

Discussion Points

1. Where does Cassie find the mysterious book?

2. Why does Hector get wet and muddy?

a) He falls into a pond

b) There is a storm

c) He is in the woods

3. What was your favourite part of the story?

4. How does Grandad get stuck at the old mill?

5. Why do you think the book's pages turn blank?

6. Who was your favourite character and why?

7. There were moments in the story when Cassie had to be **convincing**. Where do you think the story shows this most?

8. What do you think happens after the end of the story?

Book Bands for Guided Reading

The Institute of Education book banding system is a scale of colours that reflects the various levels of reading difficulty. The bands are assigned by taking into account the content, the language style, the layout and phonics. Word, phrase and sentence level work is also taken into consideration.

The Maverick Readers Scheme is a bright, attractive range of books covering the pink to grey bands. All of these books have been book banded for guided reading to the industry standard and edited by a leading educational consultant.

To view the whole Maverick Readers scheme, visit our website at

www.maverickearlyreaders.com

Or scan the QR code to view our scheme instantly!

Maverick Chapter Readers
(From Lime to Grey Band)